Paddington
the
Artist

First published in hardback in Great Britain by HarperCollins Publishers in 1985
First published in paperback by Collins Picture Books in 2000
This edition published by HarperCollins Children's Books in 2009

1 3 5 7 9 10 8 6 4 2

ISBN-13: 978-0-00-664745-4

Collins Picture Books is an imprint of HarperCollins Children's Books.
HarperCollins Children's Books is a division of HarperCollins Publishers Ltd.

Visit our website at: www.harpercollins.co.uk
Printed and bound in China

MICHAEL BOND

Paddington
the
Artist

illustrated by R.W. ALLEY

HarperCollins *Children's Books*

O ne Sunday Paddington was out for a walk
with his friend Mr Gruber, when they
came across some paintings tied to the railings
outside the park.

"It's what is known as an Outdoor
Exhibition," said Mr Gruber. "They have
one here every week when the weather
is nice."

"All the paintings are for sale," Mr Gruber explained. "This one is called 'Sunset in Bombay'."

"I'm glad I don't live in Bombay," said Paddington. "It might keep me awake all night."

"How about this one then?" said Mr Gruber.
"It's called 'Storm at Sea'."

Paddington suddenly wished he hadn't
eaten such a big breakfast.

"I feel sick," he said, and he hurried
on to the next picture.

"This is a picture the artist painted of himself," said Mr Gruber. "It's called a self-portrait. I think it looks very like him."

Paddington gave the picture a hard stare.

"I don't think I'll buy any paintings today, Mr Gruber," he said.

Paddington looked very thoughtful as he made his way back home to number thirty-two Windsor Gardens.

When he got there, Paddington collected all his paints and brushes from his room and went out into the garden.

The next Sunday, when he and Mr Gruber had finished their walk, Paddington led the way back towards Windsor Gardens.

"I'm having an Outdoor Exhibition of my own this week, Mr Gruber," he said.

"This is meant to be a sunset in Windsor Gardens. Only it took me quite a long time and it got dark before I could finish it.

"And this is a picture of a rainstorm, only it got very wet and all the paint ran."

"This is my best one," said Paddington. "It's a picture of me. I've put my special paw mark on to show I painted it myself."

Mr Gruber gazed at Paddington's portrait for a long time.

"It is very good, Mr Brown," he said at last, not wishing to upset his friend, "but I think you look even better in real life."

"I kept going upstairs to look at myself in the mirror," said Paddington, "but by the time I got downstairs again I'd forgotten what I looked like."

"Painting isn't as easy as it looks," Paddington
added sadly, "especially with paws. I think
I might give up."

"I hope you don't do that, Mr Brown,"
Mr Gruber said thoughtfully.

After Mr Gruber had said goodbye, Paddington sat down beside his paintings hoping that someone would stop and buy one.

But it was a warm day and no one came past.
In the end Paddington fell asleep.

When he woke up, Paddington found to his surprise that all his pictures had gone.

But tucked inside his duffle coat he found an envelope with his name on: Mr Paddington Brown, 32 Windsor Gardens. And inside the envelope there was some money and a note saying 'Thank you'.

If Mr and Mrs Brown recognised Mr Gruber's
writing they didn't say anything. They hadn't
had such a peaceful time for ages.

And best of all, Paddington carried on painting.
So everyone was happy.

"I think I may paint a family portrait now," said Paddington. "That is, if I have enough paint left for all the smiles."

Collect all the fantastic books about Paddington!

FICTION

A Bear Called Paddington
PB: 978-0-00-717416-4 £4.99
HB: 978-0-00-714187-6 £9.99

A Bear Called Paddington
CD Audio: £9.99
978-0-00-716165-2

More About Paddington
CD Audio: £9.99
978-0-00-716168-3

More About Paddington
PB: 978-0-00-675343-8 £4.99

Paddington Marches On
PB: 978-0-00-675362-9 £4.99

Paddington Takes the Test
PB: 978-0-00-675378-0 £4.99

Paddington Helps Out
PB: 978-0-00-675344-5 £4.99

Paddington Abroad
PB: 978-0-00-675345-2 £4.99

Paddington at Large
PB: 978-0-00-675363-6 £4.99

Paddington at Work
PB: 978-0-00-675367-4 £4.99

Paddington on Top
PB: 978-0-00-675377-3 £4.99

Paddington Takes the Air
PB: 978-0-00-675379-7 £4.99

Paddington Goes to Town
PB: 978-0-00-675366-7 £4.99

Paddington Here and Now
HB: 978-0-00-726940-2 £10.99
PB: 978-0-00-726941-9 £4.99
Audio CD:
978-0-00-727086-6 £11.99

PICTURE BOOKS

Paddington and the Grand Tour
illustrated by Bob Alley
PB: 978-0-00-712314-8 £5.99
PB & Audio CD: 978-0-00-728234-0 £7.99

Paddington
illustrated by R.W. ALLEY
HB: 978-0-00-723632-9 £10.99
PB: 978-0-00-723633-6 £5.99
PB & Audio CD: 978-0-00-725655-6 £7.99

Paddington in the Garden
illustrated by R.W. ALLEY
PB: 978-0-00-712316-2 £5.99
PB & Audio CD: 978-0-00-728233-3 £7.99

Paddington and the Christmas Surprise
illustrated by R.W. ALLEY
PB: 978-0-00-725773-5 £5.99
PB & Audio CD: 978-0-00-728236-4 £7.99

ALSO AVAILABLE

Paddington at the Carnival • PB: 978-0-00-664725-6 • £5.99
Paddington at the Zoo • PB: 978-0-00-664744-7 • £5.99
Paddington and the Marmalade Maze • PB: 978-0-00-710768-1 • £5.99
Paddington at the Palace • PB: 978-0-00-710440-6 • £5.99
Paddington's Suitcase • 978-0-00-725194-0 • £14.99
Paddington My Book of Marmalade • HB: 978-0-00-726946-6 • £5.99
A Bear Called Paddington – 50th Anniversary edition • HB: 978-0-00-726196-3 • £14.99